P9-DBN-911

THE Army of Two

THE Army of Two

by POLLY CURREN
Pictures by ROBERT SHORE

 SCHOLASTIC BOOK SERVICES
NEW YORK • TORONTO • LONDON • AUCKLAND • SYDNEY • TOKYO

This book is sold subject to the condition that it shall not be resold, lent, or otherwise circulated in any binding or cover other than that in which it is published — unless prior written permission has been obtained from the publisher — and without a similar condition, including this condition, being imposed on the subsequent purchaser.

ISBN: 0-590-00169-8

Text copyright © 1975 by Polly Curren. Illustrations copyright © 1975 by Robert Shore. All rights reserved. Published by Scholastic Book Services, a division of Scholastic Magazines, Inc.

13 12 11 10 9 8 7 6 5 4 3   01/8

Printed in the U.S.A.

For Ruth

There was a lighthouse
at the edge of the ocean.
It was tall and round
and all painted white.
And it had a bright, white light.

There was a barn out in back
and a little brown house
to go with it.

There was a lighthouse keeper, Mr. Bates,
and his wife, Mrs. Bates,
and their two daughters.
They all lived in the little brown house
in a seacoast town, long, long ago.

One girl was called Abbie.
Some called her Nabby,
but her real name was Abigail.

The other girl was Rebecca.
She was older than Abbie,
and Rebecca was always called Becky.

Abbie could dust.
Becky could sweep.
Mrs. Bates did the cooking and washing.
She did the spinning and sewing.

Keeper Bates tended
the light
up in the lighthouse tower.

There was a war going on
between England and America.
This was long, long ago
during the War of 1812.

One day in June,
when people were busy working,
two British ships came into the harbor
and set fire to the boats
anchored there.

"Fire! Fire!"
yelled the first man who saw it.
He ran through the streets
shouting, "Fire! Fire! Fire!"
at the top of his lungs.

Housewives popped their heads
out of doorways
and windows.
Bells rang.
Dogs came barking.
Men and children came running.
"Where? Where?" the people shouted.

"Down by the lighthouse,"
yelled a farmer, racing past.
"Bring your fire bucket — and come on!
All our boats are burning!"

Everyone grabbed a fire bucket
and raced to the harbor.

But it was too late.
Ten ships,
loaded with grain,
fish,
and flour
— all ready to sail —
had burned,
and every bit of food was lost.

The town people were all
as mad as wet hens.
"What a mean, mean thing to do,"
they said.
"We'll make sure the Britishers
never do that again!"

The men formed
a home-made army.
Two men were sent
to stand guard
at the tall, round lighthouse.

"No British ship will ever
steal into our harbor again,"
everybody said.

The two guards moved
into the little brown house.
They brought their clothes
and their guns.
The tall guard brought along a fife.
The other one brought a drum.

"Oh, who plays the fife?" asked Abbie.

"I do," said the tall one.

"And I play the drum," the other guard said.

"I play the fife too," said Becky.

"You do!" said the guard.

"But not very well," Abbie said.

"Abbie dear,
mind your manners!" Mrs. Bates spoke up.
"Becky plays her fife
just as well
as you beat your drum."

Abbie's face turned red.

Becky said shyly,
"Would you like us
to play a tune?"

"Sure," said the guards.

Becky played "Yankee Doodle" — but not very well.
Abbie beat the drum with all her might.

"That was fine,"
the guards said politely.
"Now we'll play
the call-to-arms
for you."

   Ta Ta TA Ra Ta Ta TA Ra
   Ta Ta Ta Ra Ta Ta Ta-aa-aa-aa-a-a
went the fifer on his fife.

And the drummer beat a loud
rolling roar of war
on his drum.

Abbie and Becky clapped
until their arms ached.

"I like that tune," Becky said.

And Abbie said, "So do I."

The two guards laughed
and one of them said,
"That's a very important tune to remember."

"Whenever you hear
the call-to-arms,"
the tall guard told them,
"it means the whole army
is marching to meet the enemy.
We'll teach you to play it
while we're here."

And they did.
That made Abbie and Becky
real proud and happy.

The men stood guard,
and the days went along.
June turned into July.
July turned into August.

The wheat and the corn
grew high in the fields
and still the British
didn't come.

Then one day
August turned into September
and it was harvest time.
Every man was needed
to help with the work in the fields.

Keeper Bates and the two guards
left their post at the lighthouse

to go into the fields
and bring in the crops.

Mrs. Bates joined all the women in town
to cook
and carry food
to the hard-working men.

Abbie and Becky
were left alone
in the little brown house
by the sea.

Becky looked out the window
and saw
a British war ship
coming into the harbor!

"Abbie!" she shouted.
"They're coming! They're coming!"

"Who?" asked Abbie.

"The Britishers!" Becky answered.

"Where?" cried Abbie.

"Out there," said Becky.
And she pointed to the harbor.

Abbie looked out the window
and saw the big British war ship
with a landing barge
in the water beside it.
British soldiers were
climbing down over the side
and into the barge,
ready to come to shore.

"Oh! Our flour boats!" Abbie cried.
"What will happen to them?
There are two boats full of flour
here in the harbor."

The barge was filled now.
The British in their bright red coats
looked like lines of stiff wooden soldiers.
The sailors were rowing for shore.

"Becky! They're getting closer!" Abbie called.
"I'm sure they're coming in
to set our flour boats on fire!"

Abbie looked frightened. She was ready to cry.
But Becky was fighting mad!

"The Britishers won't burn our ships again,"
she said.
"We have to do something
to scare them away."

"But how do you scare a soldier?" asked Abbie.
"We can't yell *Boo* at the Britishers."

"Get your drum.
We can scare them away with music," Becky said.

Abbie's feelings were hurt.
"Mind your manners, Becky," she said.
"It's not polite to make fun of my drumming."

Becky grabbed her fife.
"That's not what I mean," she said.
"I'll play my fife
and you beat your drum.
We'll play the call-to-arms."

Abbie didn't need to hear any more.
She grabbed up her drum, ready to go.
"When the Britishers hear
the call-to-arms
they will think our army
is marching here to meet them," she said.

"And that's the way that
you and I
will scare the Britishers away," Becky said
with a wide, wise smile.

Becky took her fife
and Abbie took her drum,
and they ran out the back door
of the little brown house
on that day,
long, long ago.

The barge was almost
up to the lighthouse.
There was the Captain.
There were his men.
There were the strong sailors,
pulling and pulling for shore.

Abbie and Becky hid
behind the barn,
down in back of the lighthouse.

They could still see the barge
full of British soldiers,
but the men could not see them.

Becky played her fife.
   Ta Ta TA Ra Ta Ta TA Ra
   Ta Ta Ta Ra Ta Ta Ta-aa-aa-aa-a-a

Brr-rr-rr-rrrrm
Abbie beat the roll of war
on her drum so hard
and so loud
her ears ached.

The Captain heard the call, plain as day,
and he didn't like the sound.

"Hark!" he said. "Do you hear it?
They are sounding the call-to-arms."

"Sir," a young sailor said,
"does that mean their army
is coming to meet us here?"

"That's what it means," the Captain said.
He frowned as he counted his company of soldiers.
He didn't have many men.

Ta Ta TA Ra Ta Ta TA Ra
Ta Ta Ta Ra Ta Ta Ta-aa-aa-aa-a-a
Becky tooted the call on her fife again.

Brr-rr-rr-rrrrm
Abbie beat away on her drum.

This time the call sounded much louder
to the men coming in on the barge.

"Halt! Stop the boat!"
ordered the Captain.
He looked worried.
How could his one small company
of men do battle with a whole army?

But the Captain knew what he had to do,
so he said,
"Get ready to go ashore."

"All of us, sir?" asked one young soldier.

"Right now, sir?" asked another.

And one sailor said,
"Captain, sir,
I'd rather go back
to our war ship."

Down by the barn,
Becky and Abbie watched
and giggled.

"I think we're scaring them," Abbie whispered.

"I know we are," Becky said.
"Let's play
the call-to-arms
again."

So they did.

Right in the middle
of the first "Ta Ta TA Ra . . ."
"BANG"
went a gun
on the big British war ship
in the harbor.
Up went a flag,
a signal that meant,
"Attention! Return to your ship!"

The Captain looked relieved.
His soldiers looked happy.
The sailors turned the barge around
and rowed
away from the shore of the seacoast town,
away from the tall, round lighthouse.

Becky and Abbie,
down by the barn,
watched the enemy rowing away.

"We scared the Britishers!" Abbie giggled.

"We did! We did!"
Becky laughed.
"And now we'll give them
a farewell tune."

So Becky took her fife
and played "Yankee Doodle" —
and she played it very well this time.

Abbie beat her drum
so loud
and so hard
people heard it all over town.

The British
climbed back
into their war ship
and sailed away.

That was the way
two girls
frightened the British away
and saved their boats
and their seacoast town
that day,
long, long ago.

A note from the author

Everything in this story really did happen—but not exactly the way I've told it here. There really was a lighthouse at the edge of the ocean with a little brown house beside it. The lighthouse was built in 1811 in Scituate, Massachusetts, and it still stands there today. But the great white light in the tower isn't used anymore.

Captain Simeon Bates was the keeper of the lighthouse. He tended the light that guided the ships at sea. The captain and his wife and their daughters, Abbie and Becky Bates, lived in the little brown house. They are young girls in our story, but we know that the sisters were really much older when they played the call-to-arms that day down behind the barn. I wrote about them as young girls because I thought the story would be more fun to read that way.

Abbie and Becky's adventure took place only 39 years after the American War of Independence began. England and the United States were at war again. We fought because England took sailors off our ships and would not let us trade freely with other countries. We call this the War of 1812, but the war really lasted about two and a half years.

The War of 1812 was a little more than two years old on September 1, 1814, when the Army of Two frightened the British away and saved their little town.